To Sophie, Annie, and Ralph
—D.B.

For my dearest Charlotte
—M.H.

Black Diamond & Blake

by Deborah
Blumenthal

illustrated by
Miles Hyman

ALFRED A. KNOPF
New York

nce there were crowds, and clinging jockeys, and horses to ride against in the razor-fine seconds it took to be first across the finish line. Black Diamond covered the ground like a shock wave, winning races again and again. He heard whistles, and loud hoo-rays, and the click-click of cameras as wreaths of flowers were placed around his neck.

Everyone would gather around him, eager to be his friend. While the other horses were left alone, Black Diamond's owner stroked his neck and covered him with a red velvet blanket that said "Champ." His jockey fed him sweet apples, and the stable hand smiled as he brushed his coat.

All this from his racetrack family made Black Diamond want to win every race. He was the fastest horse, the best. They were proud of him, and he would never let them down.

Week after week, the jockey rode him hard and then harder. Still, Black Diamond kept on racing, even when his knees and ankles got tired and sore. One day, he ran as hard as he could but lost the race, by just a little. "Guess he can't win them all," somebody said. Fans shook their heads as they left the racetrack. Black Diamond waited and waited for the jockey to bring him apples, but this time he just patted him and walked on.

Weeks later, another race. Black Diamond stumbled and hurt his leg. As he limped off the track, a stillness filled the stands. Moments later, there was a hissing sound, then "BOOO!" Torn tickets, like confetti, rained down from the stands. He had tried his best—didn't they understand? A doctor bandaged his leg, then left him all alone. Black Diamond snorted and neighed to get attention, kicking the stall door. After that, no one took him out to race anymore.

Soon after, a man puffing on a big cigar came to the stables with a fat wallet in his hand. He wanted to buy Black Diamond and take him far away. When the man came too close, the choking smoke and the smell of burning made Black Diamond rear up on his hind legs. Outside the stall, he heard other men talking harshly about him.

But then a gentle voice rose above the others. That man led Black Diamond to the open doors of a horse trailer painted sky blue. Where were they taking him? Why was he leaving his *home*? Black Diamond looked back once more, then stepped inside. After the doors slammed shut, he watched through a small window as his world changed to a new home among green hills.

This place had high stone walls and locks on the doors. The men were all dressed the same. Someone called them inmates, and the place a prison. Black Diamond heard someone say, "Here's a new one for the horse-care program."

The doors of the narrow trailer were flung open to blinding sunshine, and Black Diamond squinted as he was led out to begin his new life. "It'll be okay," the man with the gentle voice said, standing at Black Diamond's side. "You'll see."

At first he felt lost with no track to follow. He saw other horses, but just watched them from a distance. The hard sound of a man's voice over a loudspeaker made him jerk back. But in the stable, a man with green eyes and a quick grin came in to take care of him. His name was Blake.

Blake just watched Black Diamond for a while, and for a while Black Diamond watched him back. One morning Blake took a small step toward him, waited, then reached out and lightly stroked his head. Black Diamond didn't move, and Blake just nodded, and stroked him again and again. Then Black Diamond turned toward Blake and nudged his hip. "How did you know?" Blake laughed, pulling a cinnamon treat out of his pocket and offering it to Black Diamond. Blake always used a special voice when he spoke to Black Diamond, a voice that told him he was a friend.

Every day Blake hauled in the hay, cleaned Black Diamond's stable, and changed his water, humming and singing while he worked. Sometimes a whoosh of spray escaped from the hose like a jack-in-the-box and soaked them both. Blake would shake his head and holler, but Black Diamond didn't mind a little shower.

Once when they were alone, Blake put his face close to Black Diamond, and told him a secret. "I grew up in a family with six kids," he whispered. "Everything changed the day my dad got sick and couldn't work anymore.

"We needed help," Blake explained, shaking his head slowly. "I went to town and stole money," he went on, closing his eyes. "I knew it wasn't right, but all I could think of was helping my dad pay our bills so that they wouldn't take away our home." Black Diamond's warm brown eyes told Blake that deep down he understood.

The friends took long walks over the hills when the towering trees were green, then yellow, red, and orange, and then white with a fresh coat of snow.

Then one morning Blake came into the stable wearing a brown coat and cowboy hat. He set a suitcase down beside him.

"I have to go now," he said to Black Diamond in a gruff voice, glancing at him, then looking away. Black Diamond lifted his head and stared back with his eyes shining. He took a step toward Blake.

"Stop!" said Blake, louder than he had to. "You can't come with me. I've done my time and now I'm free." He kicked aside some hay with the tip of his boot and stared hard at the ground. "I don't have a backyard," Blake said, shaking his head. "I don't even know where I'm gonna live. I just . . . I gotta go." He grabbed his bag, quickly turned away, and left the stable.

From then on, a man named Mack came out to the stalls.
He hauled in the hay, but often he found the hayrack full
and Black Diamond standing still as a shadow, his head
hanging down. "You're getting thin, boy," Mack said.
"What's wrong with you?"

Another man named Carl did stable chores too. Carl
yanked on Black Diamond's halter and slapped him,
shouting *"GET!"* to make him go out into the field. Once,
when Carl walked behind him, Black Diamond lifted his
legs and kicked him.

For days, weeks, and months, Black Diamond looked
for Blake. Whenever there were footsteps, his head shot up,
but it was always Mack. Mack never smiled or sang. He just
did his job.

Then one day when the sun was high and the sky was water blue, within the shadow of the leafy tree where he stood, Black Diamond heard the hum of a car. The sound came closer and closer, then stopped. He saw a man standing in the distance, his hand shading his eyes. He saw him climb the fence and look all around. The man started to turn away, until Black Diamond moved from the darkness of the shade.

Suddenly, as if he heard a voice from within, Black Diamond's head shot up, and in a minute that grew heavy with time, they took each other in.

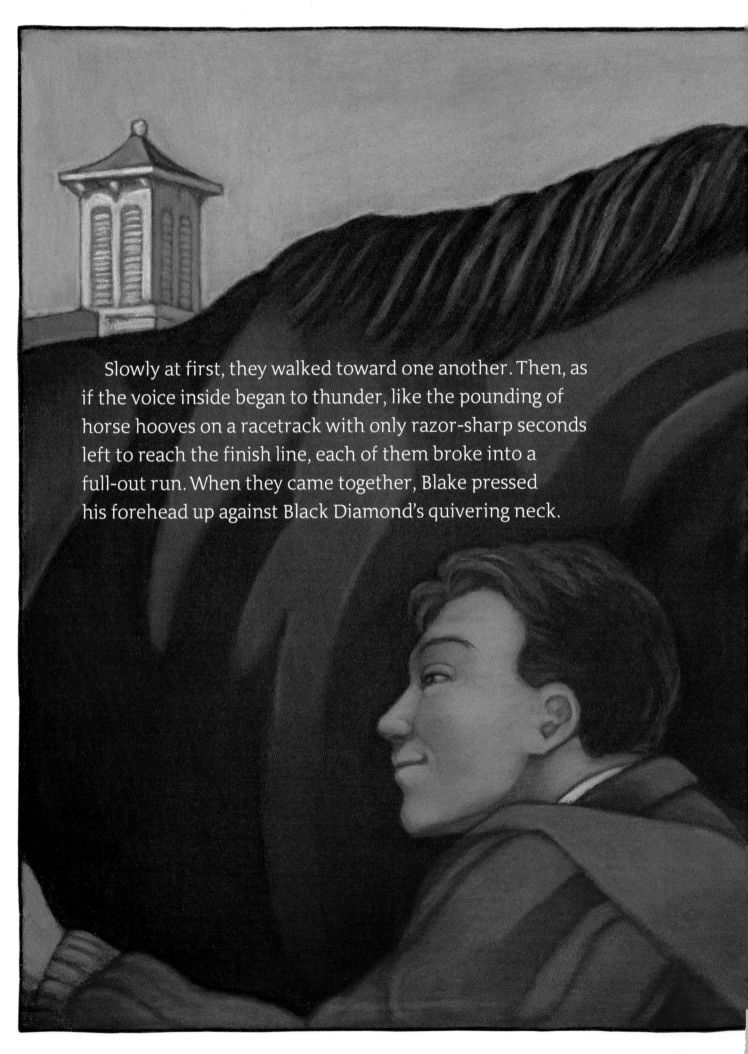

Slowly at first, they walked toward one another. Then, as if the voice inside began to thunder, like the pounding of horse hooves on a racetrack with only razor-sharp seconds left to reach the finish line, each of them broke into a full-out run. When they came together, Blake pressed his forehead up against Black Diamond's quivering neck.

In a rush, short of breath, Blake told Black Diamond about the job he'd found miles away on a horse farm. At first, he just cleaned the stables, but he worked hard and got a better job working with the trainers. Finally, he got time off and drove as fast as he could to get back to the prison.

"They're gonna let me take you with me now," Blake said. "I live in a house with a field behind it. It's not perfect, but I'll make it a good home for both of us."

After a last look back at the sun-speckled fields squared off by fences, Black Diamond clippety-clopped into the horse trailer painted sky blue. The man with the gentle voice said "Goodbye, Champ," then closed the doors. Through a small window, Black Diamond watched his world change once more.

Now he spends afternoons roaming free, grazing in green fields with tall grass that sways in time to the changing music of the wind. There is fresh hay and sunlight glinting through tall trees, and nights made dreamlike by the whistle of trains in the darkness. And there is his friend, Blake, now and forever.

Author's Note

What happens to racehorses when they lose their edge?

The lucky ones go to prison.

A *New York Times* story about inmates who cared for retired racehorses within the safety of prison pastures was the inspiration for this book. I learned that the program was started by a group of horse lovers eager to spare racehorses from the suffering and eventual slaughter many of them faced after their illustrious careers ended. I read of the deep emotional connections that some inmates made with the animals, so that in the end, men saved horses and horses saved men.

The first horse-rescue program began more than twenty years ago. Monique Koehler, the owner of a New York advertising agency, wanted to see racehorses going on to a safe and peaceful retirement off the turf. In her search for land, she found that the prison system owned thousands of unused acres. Her group, the Thoroughbred Retirement Foundation, saw the opportunity to pair animals with inmates, who would have the time to care for them. She formed a partnership with the Wallkill Correctional Facility in upstate New York and promised to design and run a vocational training program for the inmates in exchange for the prison's land and help.

Today, the program has been replicated at other prison facilities, with the largest at the Blackburn Correctional Complex in Lexington, Kentucky. Building on the Thoroughbred foundation's success, other groups have introduced work-rescue programs using dogs. In some, prisoners train puppies to become companions to the blind and handicapped. In others, troubled teens teach abandoned dogs obedience so that they can be adopted.

In the end, the programs all have a common goal: animals and humans raising each other's hopes and spirits to help them live better lives.

D.B.

THIS IS A BORZOI BOOK PUBLISHED BY ALFRED A. KNOPF

Text copyright © 2009 by Deborah Blumenthal
Illustrations copyright © 2009 by Miles Hyman

Published in the United States by Alfred A. Knopf, an imprint of Random House Children's Books, a division of
Random House, Inc., New York.

Knopf, Borzoi Books, and the colophon are registered trademarks of Random House, Inc.

Visit us on the Web! www.randomhouse.com/kids

Educators and librarians, for a variety of teaching tools, visit us at
www.randomhouse.com/teachers

Library of Congress Cataloging-in-Publication Data
Blumenthal, Deborah.
Black Diamond and Blake / by Deborah Blumenthal ; illustrated by Miles Hyman. — 1st ed.
p.   cm.
Summary: After an injury, Black Diamond, a racehorse, is sent to a country prison where he forms a strong bond
with the inmate assigned to care for him. Includes facts on programs that pair animals with prisoners who
learn how to take care of them.
ISBN 978-0-375-84003-6 (trade) — ISBN 978-0-375-94003-3 (lib. bdg.)
[1. Race horses—Fiction. 2. Horses—Fiction. 3. Prisoners—Fiction. 4. Prisons—Fiction.] 1. Hyman, Miles, ill. 11. Title.
PZ7.B6267Bl 2009
[E]—dc22
2008004980

The illustrations in this book were created using dry pastels on Sennelier pastel card.

MANUFACTURED IN CHINA

February 2009

10 9 8 7 6 5 4 3 2 1

First Edition